NOD AND AMY

Written and Illustrated
by Chen Zexin

CARDINAL
MEDIA

Nod the mouse is building a new house near his best friend Amy's home. She helps him move the stones.

They love being neighbors and
always have lots of fun together.

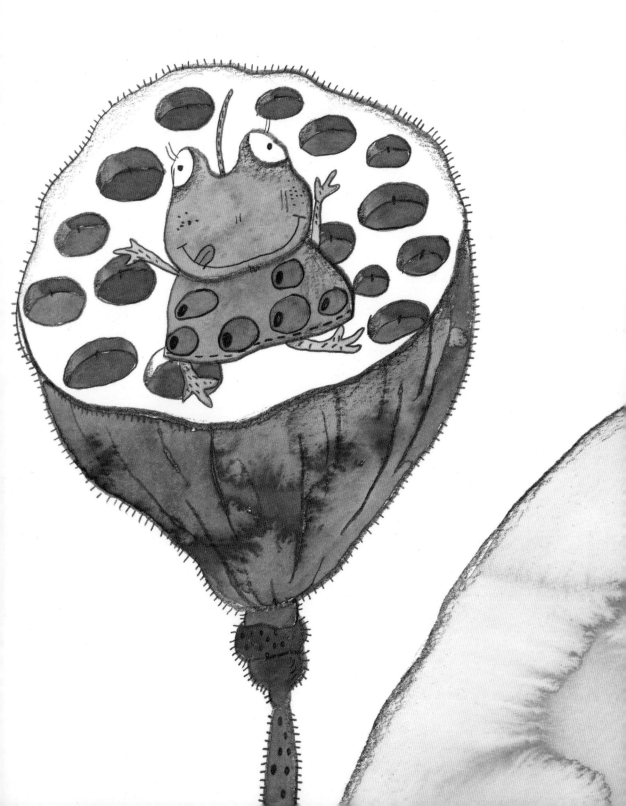

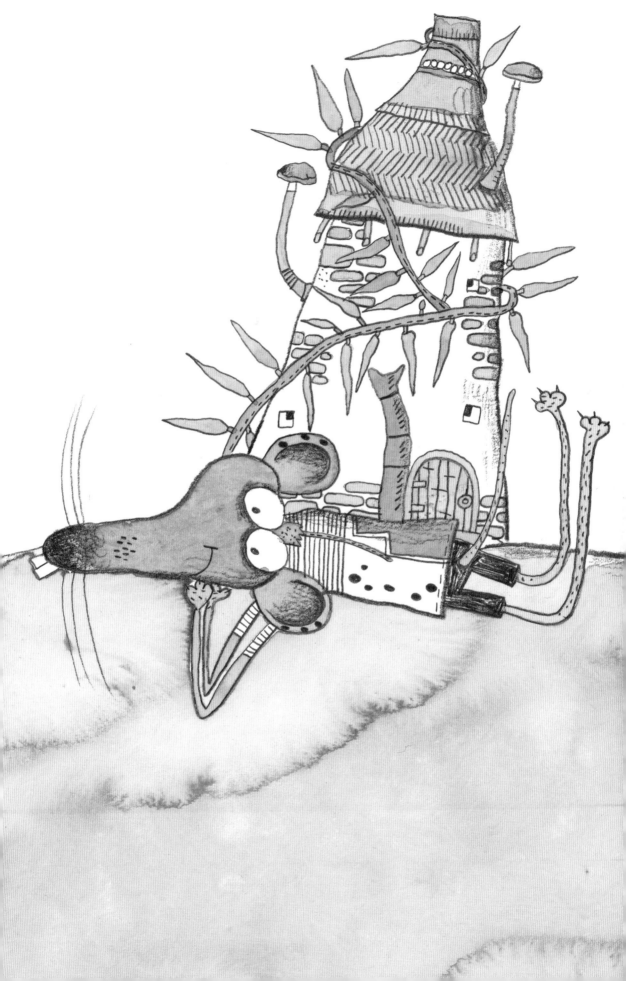

"Nod, can you hear me?"

"Yes, Amy, I can hear you clearly!"
Nod says.

In the springtime,
they love to swing.

They also go to the field to catch insects.

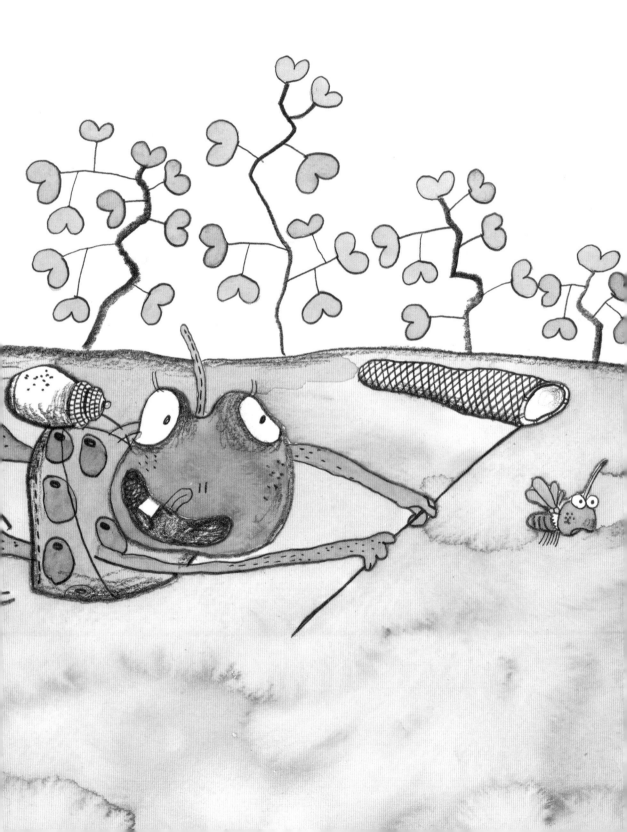

One day the two go for a long hike.
Amy can hop up on the rocks easily.

Nod's long legs help him to climb the hill.

When it starts to rain, Amy keeps them dry
with an umbrella while Nod rushes them home.

In the summer, the friends go for a swim.
Amy shows Nod the frog kick.

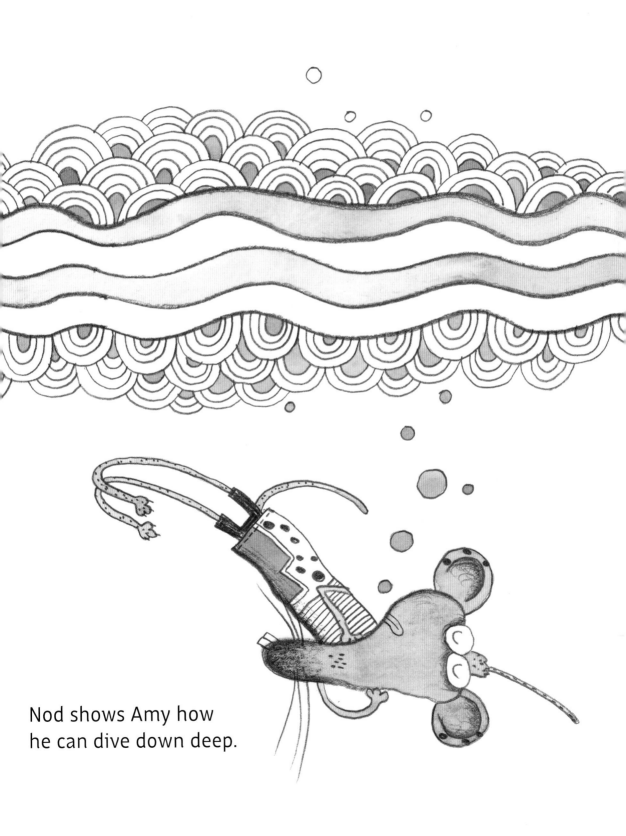

Nod shows Amy how
he can dive down deep.

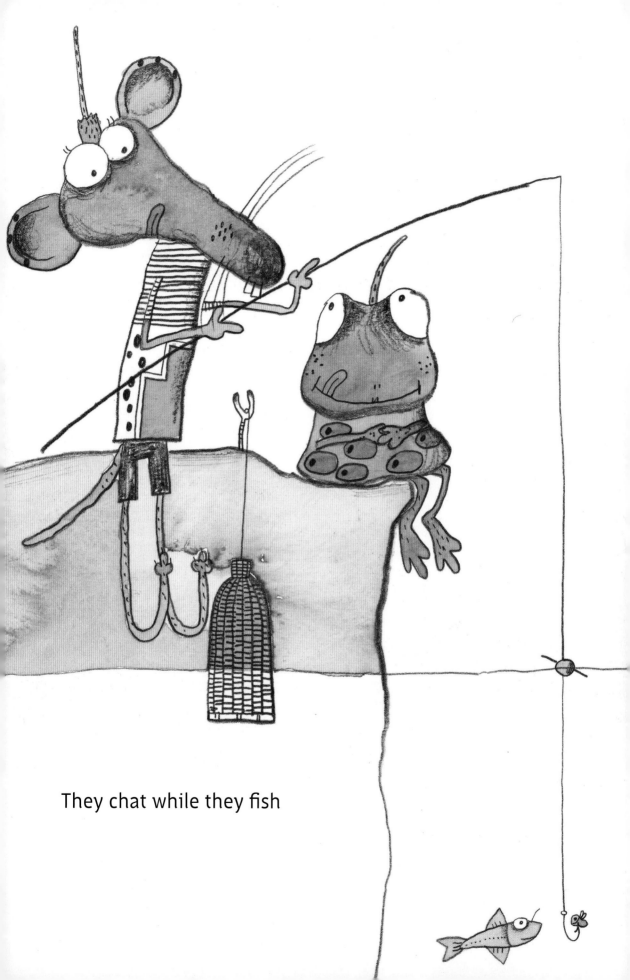

They chat while they fish

and laugh while they explore.

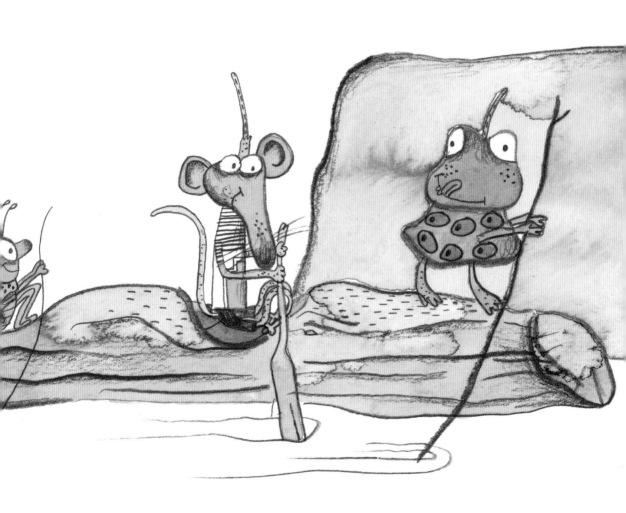

When fall winds blow, Nod and Amy dance along with the fluttering leaves.

They also play hide-and-seek in the pumpkin patch.

Friends help them move the pumpkins to Nod's house.

So Nod makes his special pumpkin pie for everyone!

One cold day, Amy digs a hole. "It's time for me to have a long sleep underground through the winter." Nod will miss playing with his friend.

But he quietly guards the entrance so that no one wakes Amy from her sweet dreams. "I'll see you in the spring, my friend!" he says.

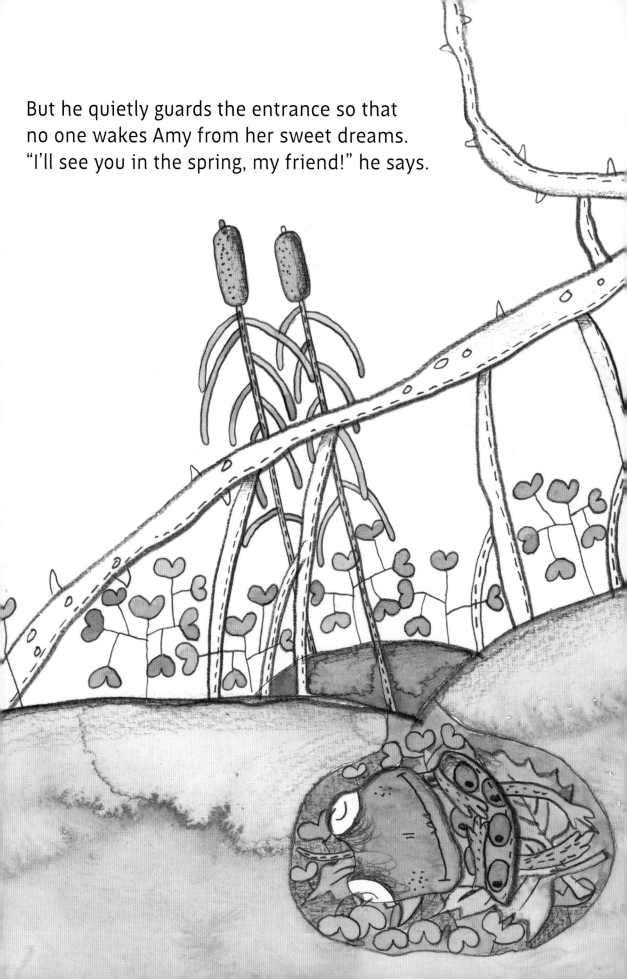